"I'm Not Sleepy"
DENYS CAZET

Orchard Books   New York

Other books by the author

Great-uncle Felix

A Fish in His Pocket

"Never Spit on Your Shoes"

Mother Night

Daydreams

 Orchard Books, 387 Park Avenue South, New York, NY 10016. Manufactured in the United States of America. Printed by General Offset Company, Inc. Bound by Horowitz / Rae. Book design by Mina Greenstein. The text of this book is set in 16 point ITC Weidemann Medium. The illustrations are pencil and watercolor drawings reproduced in full color. 10 9 8 7 6 5 4 3 2 1

Library of Congress Cataloging-in-Publication Data. Cazet, Denys. I'm not sleepy / story and pictures by Denys Cazet. p. cm. "A Richard Jackson book." Summary: Father tells a "guaranteed-to-put-anyone-to-sleep" bedtime story to Alex with humorous results. ISBN 0-531-05898-0. ISBN 0-531-08498-1 (lib. bdg.) [1. Bedtime—Fiction. 2. Sleep—Fiction. 3. Fathers and sons—Fiction.] I. Title. PZ7.C2985Im 1992 [E]—dc20 91-15958

This book is for
Happy Alex and
Grumpy Rose.

*A*lex climbed into bed.
"Have a happy sleep," said his father.
"I'm not sleepy," said Alex.

"In that case," said Father, "I'll tell you my no-matter-
how-wide-awake-you-are-I-can-make-you-sleepy
sleepy story."

Alex wiggled. "My pajamas are twisted."

"Once upon a time, there was a little boy who wasn't very sleepy, so he straightened out his pajamas and went for a walk.

"He walked over the hill and down the road, into a boily, boily jungle.

"Since he wasn't very sleepy, he walked, and walked, and walked, and walked,

until finally, he was so tired that he lay down by the
edge of the road. He closed his weary eyes and—"

Alex climbed out of bed.
"What's the matter?"
"The boily, boily jungle made me thirsty," said Alex.

He drank three glasses of water and then climbed back into bed.

Father continued.

"The little boy was very thirsty. So…he walked, and walked, and walked, until he found a pool of water.

"He drank plenty of water so he wouldn't be thirsty anymore.

"He was so tired, so very, very tired. He closed his weary eyes and—"

Alex climbed out of bed.
"Now what?"
"Too much water from the pool," said Alex.

Father waited until Alex slipped back into bed.

"Just as the little boy was about to fall asleep, a huge thingamajig came crashing through the jungle.

"The thingamajig chased the brave little boy through the jungle trees.

"It chased him up a giant pooa-pooa tree.
"The little boy climbed higher and higher.
"The thingamajig climbed closer and closer.
"When the brave little boy reached the tip-top,
he was so high, he touched the moon."

Alex pulled the covers over his head.

Father peeked under the blanket. "Do you need a drink of water?"

"I'm not thirsty," said Alex.

"Do you have to use the bathroom?"
"I already went."
"Hmm…" said Father. "Where was I?"
"On the moon," Alex said. "Hurry!"

"Just as the thingamajig reached out to grab the little boy, a shooting star swooshed by and knocked it off the tree.

"The little boy grabbed the star's tail and sailed toward the earth.

"The thingamajig cried like a baby.

"The shooting star zoomed away, and the little boy soared over fat, pillowy clouds.

"A tropical breeze lifted him gently. It carried him on and on through the dusky night.

"It carried him on and on over dark, boily jungles,

and over hills, and roads, and tiny houses.

"It carried him home.

"He drifted through the open window of his room
and tumbled softly into his bed.
"He was so tired, so very, very tired.

"The little boy closed his weary eyes. He felt cozy, and safe, and loved."

Alex closed his eyes.

"And then," whispered Father, "the little boy fell asleep."

Father waited.
The house was quiet.
He kissed Alex on the forehead, and then tiptoed across the room. "Have a happy sleep," he said softly.

"Don't forget the light," Alex whispered.